The Berenstain Bears' ®

BIRTHDAY BOY

Stan & Jan Berenstain

Reader's Digest **Kids**

Westport, Connecticut

Copyright © 1994 Berenstain Enterprises, Inc. All rights reserved. Unauthorized reproduction, in any manner, is prohibited.
Published by Reader's Digest Young Families, Inc. Printed in the U.S.A. THE BERENSTAIN BEARS is a registered trademark
of Stanley and Janice Berenstain. CUB CLUB is a trademark of Berenstain Enterprises, Inc. READER'S DIGEST KIDS &
DESIGN is a registered trademark of The Reader's Digest Association, Inc.
ISBN: O-89577-757-6

This is not a day
like any other.
It's the birthday of
my big brother.

You know my brother,
Brother Bear.
There he is,
right over there.

Yes, today's the day
we celebrate
the fact that
Brother Bear is eight.

But what's so special?

What's so great?

What's the big deal
about being eight?

I do not like
to complain,
but Brother can be
an awful pain.

He really thinks
that he's hot stuff.

Sometimes he plays
a little rough.

But I'm a little
sneaky, too.
Tickling him
is what I do.

Another complaint
I have, you see—
when something goes wrong,
he blames it on me!

But when Papa
looks him in the eye,
Brother knows better
than to lie.

Sis didn't do it.
What I really meant
was that it was
an accident!

Still, I must say
it's also true
I do some things
I shouldn't do...

Like the time I stepped
on his airplane glue.

What an awful,
yucky mess!
But I ask you,
did I confess?

No, I let *him*
take the blame,
Brother Bear
of airplane fame!

It's only fair,
I say to you,
that airplane glue
was his glue!

Yes, my big-deal Brother
is eight today.
Wow! Take a look
at this party tray!

Sometimes a brother
is sort of fun.
Sometimes I'm glad
that I've got one.

When my bow got thrown
into a tree,
it was Brother Bear
who stuck up for me.

He made that bully
climb up and get it.
He said, "Do it again
and you'll regret it."

And such wild games!
Hey! Look out! Stop!
The donkey's tail
is pinned on Pop!

YEEOWW

So many presents—

games,

books,

CHECKERS

TIDDLY WINKS

Story Time

and toys!

And much, much more—
noise, noise, noise!

Phew! The party's over.
Everything is calm again.
So now, I guess,
is the moment when...

I give the birthday boy
my birthday gift.

It's as light as a feather
and so easy to lift!

Oh, boy! Oh, boy!
This is good!
My favorite thing—
balsa wood!

For making planes!
Lots of strips, blocks, and planks!

Sister Bear,

Many, many, many thanks!

Yes, my big-deal brother
is eight today.
He's lots of trouble,
but I love him dearly anyway.